For Ina—all my love
and a tree good for climbing!

First published in Germany as *Lieselotte versteckt sich* in 2012 by Sauerländer
Published in the United States of America in August 2013
by Walker Books for Young Readers, an imprint of Bloomsbury Publishing, Inc.
www.bloomsbury.com

For information about permission to reproduce selections from this book, write to Permissions, Walker BFYR, 175 Fifth Avenue, New York, New York 10010
Bloomsbury books may be purchased for business or promotional use.
For information on bulk purchases please contact Macmillan Corporate and Premium Sales Department at specialmarkets@macmillan.com

Library of Congress Cataloging-in-Publication Data
available upon request
ISBN 978-0-8027-3402-0 (hardcover) • ISBN 978-0-8027-3403-7 (reinforced)

Printed in China by C&C Offset Printing Co., Ltd., Shenzhen, Guangdong
(hardcover) 10 9 8 7 6 5 4 3 2 1
(reinforced) 10 9 8 7 6 5 4 3 2 1

All papers used by Bloomsbury Publishing, Inc., are natural, recyclable products made from wood grown in well-managed forests. The manufacturing processes conform to the environmental regulations of the country of origin.

Millie and the Big Rescue

Alexander Steffensmeier

WALKER BOOKS FOR YOUNG READERS
AN IMPRINT OF BLOOMSBURY
NEW YORK LONDON NEW DELHI SYDNEY

Millie loved to play hide-and-seek.
So did her friends on the farm.

Even when all the good
hiding places were taken,
Millie somehow managed
to find the best spot.

Ready or not, here come the chickens.

Millie was nowhere to be found.

No one could see Millie in her hiding spot,
but Millie could see the **entire** farm!

Millie had found the best place to hide.

Maybe it was a little
too good.

Her friends
didn't give up
the search,
but Millie got tired of waiting.

"It's getting boring up
here," thought Millie, and she
decided to hide closer to home.

After a few branches,
she couldn't climb down
any farther.

Uh-oh . . . Millie was stuck.

What if
no one
found her?

Soon, the goat spotted Millie.

She was the best climber on the farm, so up she went to help.

Suddenly, a branch SNAPPED.

With a long jump, the goat saved herself and landed right next to Millie.

"How nice," Millie thought. "Company!"

The pony had a
SUPER idea.

All he needed was a
tablecloth and a plank
of wood. . . .

Before long, Millie had
A LOT of company.

In the kitchen, the farmer was
taking a cake out of the oven.

Something was strange. . . .
Where was the tablecloth? And why was it so quiet?

"Where is everyone?" the farmer asked the chickens.

When the farmer saw where the animals were, she went to the shed to get the long ladder.

"Oh my," she thought. "I've heard of cats being stuck in trees, but a whole farm?"

The farmer made it into the tree, but the rescue didn't go as planned. . . .

"Maybe our neighbor can help," the farmer said. "Chickens, hop down and get me something to write with."

They brought her a pencil and paper, and the farmer wrote one word. She rolled it up and tied the note around a chicken's neck. "Now take it next door. Hurry!"

"Since the tablecloth is already up here, we might as well have a picnic while we wait." So the farmer sent the rest of the chickens to fetch the cake and the dishes.

"This is so relaxing," the farmer said. "As long as nobody has to use the bathroom."

Millie looked up from her cup. She hadn't thought about that!

Millie waited for help to arrive.

What was taking so long?

The mail carrier was sitting in front of his house when the chicken suddenly hopped on his fence.

"Do you have a message from the farm for me?" he asked as he took a look at the paper.

"Yummy!" said the mail carrier. "Cake . . ."

When the mail carrier got to the farm, only a few chickens were running around. What were they trying to tell him?

Where was the farmer?

And where was the cake?

The farmer looked down from the tree.

"YOO-HOO!" she cried.

"We're up here!"

"Are you stuck?" asked the mail carrier.

"Yes," said the farmer. "Please get the ladder."

But the mail carrier had a better idea.

Quickly, he ran into the house and picked up the phone.

Millie and the farmer were astonished when a firefighter appeared soon after.

"We've rescued several cats from trees," said the firefighter. "But a whole farm? That's a new one."

"Thank you," said the farmer. "Can I offer you some cake?"

"That's a wonderful idea," said the mail carrier. "But where IS the cake?"

"Well . . . ," said the farmer, looking up.

"We've never had such a nice view while eating cake before," said the firefighters.

"Yes," said the farmer. "It even tastes better up here." The mail carrier agreed.

And so did Millie.